Arthur and
the Big Blow-Up

A Marc Brown ARTHUR Chapter Book

Arthur and the Big Blow-Up

Text by Stephen Krensky
Based on a teleplay by Joe Fallon

GO LAKEWOOD

Little, Brown and Company
Boston   New York   London

For my friends at WGBH

Chapter 1

• • • • • • • • • • •

"I'm open!" cried Arthur, wildly waving his arms.

He was calling from midfield. His team, Lakewood, was nearing the end of a soccer game against Estabrook. The Lakewood team included Buster, Binky, Sue Ellen, Francine, and the Brain.

Estabrook had scored first, but the lead hadn't lasted. Lakewood had tied things up at the end of the half.

Buster saw Arthur waving and waved back. "Oh," he realized suddenly, "Arthur wants me to pass."

Buster kicked the ball downfield to

1

Arthur. Arthur took a step back to get it, but the ball sailed over his head. He had no chance to reach it.

But Francine did. As the ball hit the ground, Francine trapped it neatly and turned toward the opposing goal. Two defenders were darting toward her. Francine waited until they were close enough, then she faked them out and dribbled past them.

The Brain was waiting at the far goalpost. He gave Francine a small nod. Francine nodded back. Leaning forward, she chipped the ball toward the goal.

The goalie leaped up with her arms extended, but the ball escaped her grasp. Seeing his chance, the Brain jumped forward and headed the ball toward the net.

Score! Lakewood now led, 2–1.

Prunella and Fern cheered from the sidelines.

"I knew we'd get ahead," said Fern. "I just knew it. We haven't lost a game yet."

Prunella nodded. "Everybody's playing so well. And there's really good team-work. If we can keep it up, we'll win the championship for sure!"

Fern cheered. "Then it's on to the Super Bowl," she squealed.

Prunella shook her head. "There's no Super Bowl in soccer, Fern. That's football."

"No?" Fern shrugged. "Well, the World Series, then. The Fall Classic. The —"

"Fern, there's no World Series, either. That's baseball."

Fern frowned. "Well, where do we go for soccer?"

"The World Cup," said Prunella. "Or the Olympics."

"Okay. Sounds good to me."

Tweeeeet!

The whistle from the referee signaled the end of the game.

As everybody on both teams shook hands, Sue Ellen caught up with Binky. "If we win one more game, we make the play-offs," she said.

Binky smiled. "No problem," he said. "We've got a tough team at midfield."

"Binky, *you* play midfield."

"Uh-huh. Exactly."

Buster came running up to the Brain and clapped him on the shoulder.

"You really used your head on that last one," he said.

The Brain grinned. "Buster, I can always count on you to say just the right thing."

Buster beamed. "Nobody can beat us as long as we have you and Francine."

"That's right," said Arthur. "Francine did a great job setting up the score."

"Thanks, Arthur," said Francine. "You played a good game, too."

Fern ran up with a camera.

"Let me get a shot for the school news-paper."

The team gathered around the Brain and Francine, shuffling into position.

"Say, 'Armadillo with a pillow,'" Fern told them.

"ARMADILLO WITH A PILLOW!" they shouted, laughing.

Fern snapped the picture.

Chapter 2

• • • • • • • • • • • •

Even though the team was doing well, everyone knew how important it was to keep practicing. So they got together the next afternoon to scrimmage.

The team split into two groups. Francine was the captain of one. The Brain led the other.

Buster kicked the ball downfield. It bounced off Arthur's stomach and landed near his feet.

"Arthur, I'm open!" cried Francine.

Arthur's stomach hurt, but he took a deep breath and kicked the ball toward her.

"Nice pass," said Francine, taking the ball. She began dribbling down the sideline.

"Hey, out of bounds!" shouted the Brain, running over.

"I am not!" Francine insisted. "Look at my foot!"

The Brain pointed at the line. "Your foot was over the line. You just moved it back."

"No way! Your eyes are playing tricks on you to make up for the fact that I'm better than you are."

The Brain stiffened. "There's nothing wrong with my eyes. You're the one who can't see right."

"Oh, yeah?"

This argument went on and on. The other players sat down to wait it out, all except Binky. He remained standing, bouncing the ball on his head.

"Three thousand four hundred seventy-eight . . . three thousand four hundred

8

seventy-nine . . . three thousand four hundred eighty . . ."

"I wish I'd brought a book," said Buster.

Arthur yawned. He looked over at Francine and the Brain, who showed no signs of letting up.

"That's not true."

"It is."

"Hey, guys!" said Arthur. "I've got this amazing idea. What do you say we finish the game?"

Binky caught the ball. "Yeah," he said, "my head's getting sore."

The Brain folded his arms. "Obviously, we're not going to settle this ourselves. We need an arbitrator."

"A what?" asked Francine.

"A kind of judge. Someone we trust." He looked around. "You saw what happened, Arthur. You make the call."

"Me?"

"That's right."

9

Arthur tried to think back. "Well, at first it looked like her foot was over the —"

"Come on!" said Francine. "Arthur wears glasses. Are you going to trust what he sees?"

"Now, now," said the Brain, "let's be fair. Arthur is honest and trustworthy." He put his arm around Arthur's shoulders. "Why, there's no better kid in the whole school. Go on, Arthur, tell Francine she was out of bounds."

Arthur shifted his eyes from side to side. The Brain was grinning at him from one direction, and Francine was frowning from the other.

Francine sighed. "All right, Arthur, you get to decide — but don't just agree with the Brain because boys always stick together."

Arthur hesitated. "But then," he said, "it looked like her foot wasn't . . ."

The Brain's smile faded. "Oh, so now you're going to stick up for her."

"Let him speak, Brain," said Francine. "Go ahead, Arthur."

"Uh-oh," said Binky, cupping his ear with his hand. "That's my mom calling. I've got to go home for dinner."

"Can't you wait a little?" asked Arthur. "You have the only ball."

Binky laughed. "I never wait when dinner is ready." He ran off with the ball under his arm.

"Without a ball," said Buster, "the game is over."

"Then I guess it doesn't matter who's right anymore," said Arthur. He stepped out from between his two feuding friends. "I think I'll go home, too."

Within a minute, everyone had left, everyone except Francine and the Brain. They just stood there glaring at each other.

And neither of them spoke a word.

Chapter 3

• • • • • • • • • • •

The next afternoon in class, Buster nudged Arthur in the side.

"Francine and the Brain are still mad at each other," he whispered.

"Really? I never thought it would last this long."

"It's still going strong," said Buster. "You should have seen them at the beginning of lunch. They were fighting over a bowl of pistachio pudding. It was the last one, and neither of them wanted to give it up."

"What happened?"

"The pudding ended up flying through

the air and landing on Mr. Haney's arm. It was not a pretty sight."

"Was he mad?" asked Arthur. "Mr. Haney, I mean."

Buster looked a little uncomfortable. "Well, he would have been, I'm sure. But he just thought I'd sneezed on him. So he told me to use a handkerchief. Then he left as quickly as possible."

"That was lucky for them," said Arthur. "But they can't count on always being saved like that."

He looked over as Francine accidentally dropped a pencil on the floor. It rolled in front of the Brain's foot.

"Muffy, could you hand me that pencil?" she asked.

Muffy frowned. "Why don't you ask the Brain? He's closer."

"The Brain can't see feet very well," said Francine. "How's he going to see the pencil?"

The Brain snorted. "Muffy, tell Francine that I see just fine."

"Francine," said Muffy, "the Brain sees just fine. Which is why he's going to pick up your pencil."

"I'm afraid not," said the Brain. "It would be unwise for me to touch it. If I did, I might catch something nasty from Francine."

"Like what?" asked Muffy.

The Brain shuddered. "Like whatever makes her so *Francine-y.*"

"*Hmmmph!*" snorted Francine, turning away.

"Double *hmmmph!*" said the Brain.

"Quiet down," said Mr. Ratburn, calling for everyone's attention. "It's time for the speed quiz."

The class groaned.

Mr. Ratburn went right on talking. "No comments, please. You knew this was coming. Just take one quiz and pass the rest around."

He gave out a few piles. The Brain took his and was about to pass on the rest when he realized he was giving his pile to Francine. Abruptly, he turned to pass the papers to Fern on his left.

"Hey!" said Francine.

The Brain paid no attention. Francine had to wait for other copies to work their way around to Muffy, who was sitting next to her.

"Here you go, Francine," said Muffy, handing her the last one.

"What about me?" Arthur whispered. He was sitting behind Francine and the quizzes had never reached him.

"Why don't you ask your friend the Brain?" Francine suggested.

"*Pssst!* Brain! *Pssst!*"

"No talking allowed during the quiz," said Mr. Ratburn. "You have one minute. Please begin."

Arthur looked around. Everyone else was hard at work. He raised his hand, but Mr. Ratburn had his back turned.

"Mr. Ratburn," he called out finally, "I, um, think . . ."

"Time's up."

Everyone stopped writing.

Arthur leaned over to Buster. "If Francine and the Brain don't make up soon, I'll never make it to fourth grade."

Chapter 4

· · · · · · · · · · · ·

Later that afternoon, Arthur and Buster slowly walked home from school. Their heads were down. Their shoulders were slumped. Both of them were wearing their soccer uniforms, although it was hard to tell because they were covered with mud.

"It was a disaster," said Buster.

"A catastrophe," Arthur added.

"A tragedy."

"A real misfortune."

"All in all," Buster finished, "it was just bad."

They were talking about the soccer game they had just played. Lakewood had lost, 5–1, and it had never even felt close.

"The first few minutes went well," Buster said brightly. "Sue Ellen scored on that cross shot. And Binky stopped that big guy from getting through."

"Yeah," agreed Arthur, "but then . . ." He shuddered at the memory.

"Remember when I said that I hoped Francine and the Brain weren't too mad to play together?" said Buster.

"Yes," said Arthur. "And I said they would never let a little thing like an argument hurt our chances of winning. Boy, was I wrong."

Buster nodded. Francine had refused to pass to the Brain the entire game. At least three times he had been wide open in front of the goal, waving his arms to get her attention. Buster could tell that Francine had seen the Brain waving — but she had ignored him every time. Instead, she had passed to Arthur, who had been immediately swarmed by the opposing players.

Arthur sighed. "I lost the ball twice. And both times the other team scored."

"It wasn't your fault," Buster told him. "You never had a chance. But I'm really worried now. If Francine and the Brain stay mad at each other, we'll never win another game."

Arthur sighed. "And we won't make the playoffs."

They shared a worried look.

"We have to remind them how much they used to like each other," said Buster.

"I read this story once," said Arthur. "It was about two friends who got really mad at each other. It was kind of a misunderstanding, but they were both too stubborn to admit it."

"Did the story have a happy ending?" asked Buster.

"Not until both of them had traveled around the world and had saved each other from a hurricane, a swarm of killer bees, and an erupting volcano."

"We don't have time for that," said Buster. "Besides, we can't afford to send Francine and the Brain on a big trip."

"I know," said Arthur. "But we still need a plan." Arthur stopped to think. "Maybe it would help if they played something just for fun, something far from the competition of soccer."

"Good idea!" said Buster. "If we can remind them why they were such good friends in the first place, they'll patch things up for sure."

Arthur frowned. "Of course, we'll have to get them together first."

"That won't be easy," said Buster. "They may not want to spend any time together."

"In that case," said Arthur, "we just won't tell them until it's too late."

Chapter 5

• • • • • • • • • • •

"What's *he* doing here?" Francine asked Arthur as she pointed to the Brain.

"Um, didn't I mention the Brain was coming?"

"No, you didn't. I would have remembered that."

Arthur tried to laugh, but it came out as more of a gurgle. "I must be getting old," he said. "I'm sure I meant to say something about it."

The Brain was no happier to see Francine than she was to see him. "Buster, you never said *she'd* be here."

Buster scratched his head. "I didn't?

Imagine that! Funny how these things can slip your mind."

They were all standing in Buster's basement, in front of his Ping-Pong table.

"I'm leaving," said Francine.

"Count me out," agreed the Brain.

"Come on," said Arthur, "you two can't leave yet. We thought we'd play some doubles."

"Nice and relaxing," Buster added. "Brain, you and I will be one team. Arthur and Francine will be the other."

Arthur took Francine by the shoulders and led her to one side of the table.

Buster led the Brain to the other.

"Ping-Pong is fun," said Buster. "Isn't it, Arthur?"

"I'll say!" Arthur answered brightly. "Don't you agree, Francine?"

"Oh, sure," she said dully. "Fun."

"What about you, Brain?" asked Buster.

"Very amusing."

"And good exercise, too," said Arthur. "How 'bout I serve?"

The ball crossed the net and hit the Brain's unmoving paddle. It came back over the net and bounced once.

Francine slammed it back to him.

"Oh, yeah?" snapped the Brain. He didn't care what happened when Arthur served, but he was not about to let Francine get the better of him.

He returned her slam with one of his own.

The ball whizzed back and forth. Arthur and Buster stepped aside to watch.

"Well, they're playing together," said Buster.

"True," said Arthur. "But I'm not sure they're having fun."

Francine and the Brain finally stopped. Both were out of breath and leaned heavily on the table.

"Whose point?" gasped Francine.

The Brain took a deep breath. "Don't know. The ball appears to have vaporized."

"You know," said Arthur, "it's getting a little stuffy in here. Maybe we should go outside."

"That's right," said Buster. "Sunshine. Fresh air." He took a deep breath. "Last one to the tree house is a rotten egg."

Before Arthur or Buster could make another move, Francine and the Brain ran up the stairs and out the door, and headed for Arthur's house.

A few minutes later Arthur and Buster approached the tree house. They could hear the arguing from half a block away.

"No way were you first!" snapped Francine.

"If we had the proper video recording equipment," said the Brain, "I would prove it to you."

Francine sniffed at the air. "I smell an

egg." She took a step toward the Brain and sniffed again. "A rotten egg."

"Well, so do I! And you're the source."

"Oh, really?"

Francine turned to Arthur. "Sorry, I can't stay," she said. "The smell is overpowering."

"Buster," said the Brain, "*my* olfactory senses are overwhelmed. I'll see you later."

He stalked off in one direction. Francine marched away in another.

Arthur and Buster watched them go.

"You *had* to mention the eggs," said Arthur.

Buster sighed. "It seemed like a good idea at the time."

"Any other good ideas?" Arthur asked.

"Not at the moment," Buster admitted.

Then they both sat down to think.

Chapter 6

. . . .

That evening, Arthur and his father played chess in the living room.

"I think I'll put my knight here," said Mr. Read. "He's always looking for a little adventure."

Arthur didn't stop to think. He just pushed a pawn forward.

"Are you sure you want to do that?" his father asked. "I'm threatening to take your rook."

"Huh?" Arthur took a good look at the board. "Oh," he said, "you're right."

He considered a different move.

"Knights? Rooks?" said D.W., who was watching from the side. "Chess would be much better with a few flashing lights and some sound effects."

Her father smiled. "The game has survived more than a thousand years without them, D.W. I'm not sure you'll be able to get flashing lights and sound effects to catch on." He glanced at Arthur, who was staring into space.

"Arthur, you don't seem to have your mind on the game. Is anything wrong?"

"I'm worried about Francine and the Brain." He explained what had happened. "It doesn't seem like they will ever be friends again. And I'm friends with both of them, so I feel caught in the middle."

His father nodded. "I realize that things look pretty serious. But a lot of things look that way at first."

"What can I do?" Arthur asked.

"Be patient. Francine and the Brain don't really want to be enemies. It will just take some time for them to realize that."

"But that's the problem. We don't have much time. The playoffs are next week."

"Never mind all that," said D.W. "We have something *really* important to work on."

Arthur looked puzzled. "What do you mean?" he asked.

"Don't tell me you've forgotten," said D.W. "You promised to help me write a letter to Santa."

"In May? Santa might not even be around in May. He could be on vacation."

"Then my letter will be waiting for him when he gets back. Think about it, Arthur. Santa must get a ton of letters in December. Now's the time to write — if I want to get his attention."

She pulled out some paper and a pen.

"I'll leave you two to your work," said

their father. "Arthur, we can finish our game later." He got up and went into the kitchen.

"All right, D.W., how do you want to start?"

"How about, 'Dear Santa, is it tough being the world's most handsome man?'"

Arthur looked at her in disbelief. "That's your beginning?"

She nodded. "It's always nice to start with something positive. Now where was I? 'You must be tired of hearing nice things said about you, because you hear them so often. So I'll just skip over that part. I know your time is valuable.'"

Arthur rolled his eyes, but then he just started to write.

"'Now, Santa,'" D.W. continued, "'there were just a few little problems with the presents you brought last year.'"

Arthur checked his watch. He could see it was going to be a long night.

Chapter 7

• • • • • • • • • • •

The next soccer game was two days later. Arthur and Buster had tried to use that time to get Francine and the Brain back on speaking terms. However, they had made no progress.

"Come on, you guys," Arthur said to Francine and the Brain. "The game's going to start in a few minutes. If we don't win a game soon, we won't make the playoffs."

The two former friends folded their arms and stared in opposite directions.

"I don't think you're listening," Buster put in. "Arthur said, 'WE WON'T MAKE THE PLAYOFFS.'"

To make the point clearer, Buster grabbed his throat with both hands and stuck his tongue out the side of his mouth. He staggered around and fell to the ground with a loud groan.

Francine and the Brain walked away without saying a word.

"I think that convinced them," said Buster.

"I hope so," said Arthur. "I certainly wouldn't want to see it again."

But their hopes were dashed during the game itself. Once, Francine and the Brain fought over the ball — and an opposing player stole it away. Another time, Francine refused to pass to the Brain and chipped to Buster. Before Buster could do anything, two players rushed by him, spinning him around so fast they left his ears twisted.

The Brain came running up.

"Why didn't you pass to me? I was *sooooo* open."

Francine turned to Sue Ellen. "I think the wind is picking up. I suddenly feel a big blast of hot air."

But the Brain got back at her later when Francine was wide open at the net. Instead of passing to her, he passed to Arthur.

"Here we go again," said Arthur, as the other team surrounded him.

After the game, Arthur and Buster retreated to the tree house. Arthur lay on the floor while Buster tried to untwist his ears.

"I'm getting killed out there," said Arthur, staring at the ceiling. "I'm not sure I'll survive another game."

"Ow!" said Buster, finally getting his ears separated. "We only have one game — and one chance — left. Ouch, ouch. We have to win it."

"But that game is against Mighty Mountain," said Arthur, "the strongest team in the league." He looked at Buster.

"We're doomed," they said together.

"Who's doomed?" said D.W., appearing at the top of the ladder.

"We are," said Arthur. "I'm not going to live through our next game."

"Really?" D.W. looked concerned. "That's terrible."

"I wish I had a sister who cared about me the way D.W. cares about you," said Buster.

"Oh, it's not that," D.W. explained. "I just want to make sure we get my letter to Santa finished."

Arthur groaned. "D.W., why don't you just *call* Santa?"

"For one thing, I don't have his phone number. For another, a letter is better because I can get my thoughts organized on paper and say everything right."

"On paper," Arthur murmured. He smiled and turned to Buster.

"That's it!"

They huddled together as Arthur explained what he was thinking.

"Hey!" said D.W. "I'm still here. Remember me? The little girl whose heart may be broken at Christmas. HEY!"

But the boys were too busy to notice her.

Chapter 8

· · · · · · · · · · · ·

Inside the library, the Brain sat at a table, surrounded by books. Arthur was sitting with him.

"Say it again," said the Brain.

"I want you to write Francine a letter."

The Brain laughed. "That's what I thought you said." He shook his head. "And just why would I do that?"

"Look," said Arthur, "it's pretty clear these days that when you two are near each other, you get on each other's nerves. But I know that deep down you'd like to patch up the friendship."

"Hmmmph!" said the Brain.

"Come on, Brain. When people get upset, they say things they don't mean. And then one thing leads to another."

"So?"

"That's what makes a letter so perfect. You can write everything calmly and clearly — and without interruption."

"True," the Brain admitted. "And letter-writing has a long and proud literary history."

"Exactly," said Arthur. "This way you can tell Francine how you really feel."

"That would be satisfying," the Brain said.

Arthur handed him a pencil and paper. "Go to it," he said.

Meanwhile, Buster was having a similar conversation at Francine's house.

"It sounds like a big waste of time to me," said Francine.

"No, no, no," said Buster. "You're look-ing at it all wrong."

"I am?"

"Absolutely. This is your chance to im-press the Brain with your logic, your great insights."

"Insights, huh? I like the sound of that."

"And besides," Buster added, "he won't get a chance to interrupt."

"Give me that paper!" said Francine.

"That's the spirit!" said Buster. "Share your thoughts."

"Don't worry," said Francine. "I won't leave anything out."

A little later, Buster met Arthur in the tree house.

"I've got Francine's letter!" said Buster. He handed it to Arthur.

"And I've got the Brain's," said Arthur.

He unfolded both letters and started to read Francine's aloud.

"'Dear Brain, Buster has convinced me to share my thoughts with you. In case you were wondering, I still want to be friends.'"

"That's a good start," said Buster.

Arthur continued reading. "'Now, everyone knows you are very smart, and that you think long and hard before you do stuff. However, that only makes it harder to explain why you've been so pigheaded lately. As someone who is good with words, you might prefer 'stubborn,' but I truly think 'pigheaded' suits you.'"

"Uh-oh," said Arthur.

"Maybe the Brain's is better," Buster said hopefully.

Arthur looked through it quickly. "Listen to this."

"'Francine, I realize you may have no aspirations to be a scholar, but I previously thought that you possessed at least a reasonable amount of common sense.

However, events of late have caused me to revise that estimation. To put it in words you can understand: What's your excuse for acting so dumb all the time?'"

"No more," said Buster, sagging against the wall.

Arthur joined him. "I really thought they would cooperate."

Buster shuddered. "These letters will only make things worse."

"We're doomed."

"That's for sure," said Arthur. He thought for a moment. "But we're not done yet. I have an idea. If they won't co-operate on their own, then we'll just have to do their cooperating for them."

Chapter 9

• • • • • • • • • • •

As the Lakewood team was warming up for the big game, the Mighty Mountain team got off the bus.

"Look how big they are!"

"I'll bet they eat raw meat by the light of a full moon."

Francine was stretching out her legs as Buster handed her a letter.

"What's this?" she asked.

"It's a letter from the Brain. You wrote him one, remember? He, um, wrote you back."

Buster watched Francine as she began reading.

"What do you think?" he asked.

"Hold on. I'm not done yet. Hmmmm . . . okay."

"So?" Buster looked at her closely.

"Well," said Francine, "I accept his apology. I mean, it's hard not to when someone calls you 'a blaze of glory' and 'the shooting star of the team.'"

"That does sound nice," Buster agreed. "It probably took him a very long time to think up something like that."

"You think? Knowing the Brain, he might have just dashed it off."

Buster shook his head. "I know for a fact that writing that kind of stuff takes a while."

"I guess. There's only one thing bothering me."

"Oh?" Buster looked nervous. "What's that?"

"I can't believe the Brain spelled 'soccer' s-o-k-k-e-r."

"Ah, well," said Buster, with a nervous laugh. "I wouldn't think about that too much. He was probably in a hurry to get the letter to you and he missed a few things."

Farther down the field, the Brain was running in place.

"Thirty more seconds," he told Arthur, who had come up beside him. "Then three minutes of stretching. You should do this, too, Arthur. Proper muscle conditioning is a key ingredient in playing to your full potential."

"If you say so," said Arthur. "By the way, I have a letter for you. Francine wrote it."

He handed it over.

The Brain read for a few seconds. Then he suddenly stopped running.

"This is ridiculous," said the Brain. "I refuse to give in to her demands."

"What?"

"'I want blue footie pajamas and the blond Missy Mallrat,'" the Brain read aloud. He frowned. "I'm not buying Francine any presents."

"Oh. Uh . . . ," said Arthur. "Of course you're not. That's D.W.'s Christmas list. I'm helping her out, and somehow Francine must have used her paper by mistake. Look on the other side."

The Brain flipped it over and started reading again.

"Ah . . . much better. 'I don't know what I was thinking to argue with someone of such superior intelligence.'"

"You like that, huh?"

"I'm not one to hold a grudge, Arthur. If Francine has seen the error of her ways, I can accept that."

Arthur was glad to hear it.

The referee suddenly blew the whistle. The game was about to begin.

Chapter 10

•••••••••••••

As the players took their positions, the Brain and Francine shook hands. After that, there was no stopping them.

The Brain made a long downfield pass to Francine, who kicked it in for a goal.

A few minutes later, Francine faked her way past two opponents. She crossed the ball toward the Brain, who headed it into the net.

The Mighty Mountain team never had a chance.

After the final whistle blew, the Lakewood team lifted Francine and the Brain onto their shoulders.

"Hooray for Francine!"

"Hooray for the Brain!"

"Playoffs, here we come!"

"You know, Francine," said the Brain, "your letter was right. Just because I have superior intelligence doesn't mean we can't be friends."

"Yeah — what? I didn't write that. So what else was in the letter?"

The Brain told her.

"And what about what *you* wrote?" said Francine. She rattled off a few compliments.

"I wrote no such things!" he insisted.

"Then who?"

They looked around.

"Arthur!" they shouted together.

Once their teammates put them down, they ran after him.

"Arthur," said Francine, "we know you and Buster wrote those letters."

Arthur could see there was no use in

denying it. "Sorry. It was the only thing we could think of. But now that you've been friends for a game, can't you wait until after the playoffs to be mad at each other again?"

"We're not mad at each other anymore," the Brain informed him.

Arthur looked relieved.

"We're mad at you," said Francine.

"Oh."

Francine and the Brain walked off together.

"That Arthur always thinks he knows what's best," said Francine. "What a buttinsky!" She laughed.

The Brain nodded. "However, he's a buttinsky who means well."

Francine considered this. "True," she said. "No argument there."

Then they both smiled.